# THE NUTCRACKER

LITTLE SIMON

An imprint of Simon & Schuster Children's Publishing Division

1230 Avenue of the Americas, New York, New York 10020

First Little Simon hardcover edition September 2016

Copyright © 2016 by New York City Ballet Incorporated

All rights reserved, including the right of reproduction in whole or in part in any form.

LITTLE SIMON is a registered trademark of Simon & Schuster, Inc., and associated colophon is a

trademark of Simon & Schuster, Inc. For information about special discounts for bulk purchases,

please contact Simon & Schuster Special Sales at 1-866-506-1949 or business@simonandschuster.com.

The Simon & Schuster Speakers Bureau can bring authors to your live event.

For more information or to book an event contact the Simon & Schuster

Speakers Bureau at 1-866-248-3049 or visit our website at www.simonspeakers.com.

Designed by Angela Navarra and Chani Yammer

Manufactured in China 0716 SCP

2 4 6 8 10 9 7 5 3 1

This book has been cataloged with the Library of Congress.

ISBN 978-1-4814-5829-0 (hc)

ISBN 978-1-4814-5830-6 (eBook)

# THE NUTCRACKER

Illustrated by Valeria Docampo

Based on the New York City Ballet production of *George Balanchine's The Nutcracker*®

LITTLE SIMON

New York London Toronto Sydney New Delhi

It was Christmas Eve at the Stahlbaums' house, and like children everywhere, Marie and Fritz were so excited that they could feel their toes tingle. Their parents were decorating the Christmas tree before the big holiday party, and Marie and Fritz were not allowed into the great room until it was done. They jostled each other to sneak a peek at the glittering tree through the keyhole.

At last the guests arrived, and the doors were thrown open. "Let the party begin!" everyone cried as they joyfully filled the festive room.

The children danced and played, and everyone was merry until . . .
the lights flickered and the room grew dark. A mysterious man with a
young boy entered from the shadows. The man was dressed all in black,
with a huge fluttering cape. The children scurried to hide behind their
parents just as he paused and flung back his cape over his shoulder.

Ah, there was nothing to fear. It was just Herr Drosselmeier, Marie's beloved godfather! Marie flew into his arms for a hug and shyly met his young nephew.

Herr Drosselmeier was a toy inventor, and a visit from him was always full of surprises. The curious children, their eyes full of wonder, gathered around three huge boxes he had brought with him. Suddenly the boxes sprang open, and out leaped one life-size doll, then another, and then another. The dolls danced for the delighted crowd.

As the celebration continued, Herr Drosselmeier beckoned to Marie. He had a special gift for her: a nutcracker! The Nutcracker was dressed as a handsome soldier with a white beard. Herr Drosselmeier showed Marie how the Nutcracker could open and snap his mouth to crack nuts for everyone. *Crack, crack!*

Marie was enjoying cracking nuts and passing them out to the children when suddenly jealous Fritz swooped in and snatched the Nutcracker from her. He swung it around the room and smashed it down onto the floor with a loud *bang*. Marie burst into tears. Her beloved Nutcracker was broken!

But Herr Drosselmeier knew just how to fix the Nutcracker. He tied a
scarf around the Nutcracker's head like a bandage and handed him back
to Marie, who cradled him in her arms. Then Herr Drosselmeier's nephew
gave Marie a tiny bed that was the perfect size for a nutcracker, and Marie
nestled him in it to rest.

The party was coming to a close, and everyone joined in for one last grand dance. When the music ended, the guests bundled up and made their way out into the frosty night air.

Marie waved good-bye to her dear godfather and his handsome nephew. It had been a long evening, and it was time for bed.

During the night, Marie awoke, remembering that the Nutcracker was alone downstairs in his bed. She ran down to scoop him up. With the Nutcracker safely in her arms, she curled up on the sofa and drifted back to sleep in the soft glow of the Christmas tree.

She hadn't been asleep for long when Herr Drosselmeier slipped back into the house to properly mend the Nutcracker. He gently slid him out of Marie's arms, repaired him under the light of the moon, and disappeared into the darkness.

But then strange things began to happen. At the stroke of midnight, Marie was pulled from her sleep by the clock chimes. She rubbed her eyes in surprise. Great big mice appeared from the shadows and began to scurry across the room.

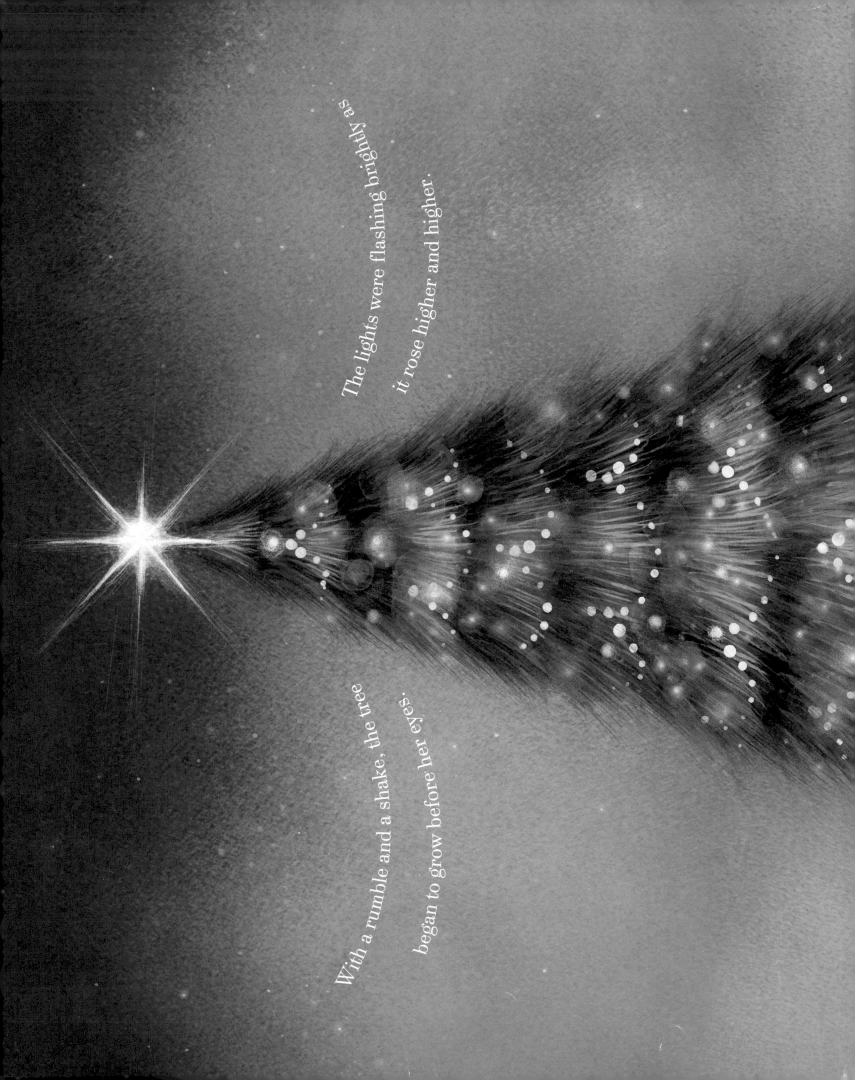

The lights were flashing brightly as it rose higher and higher.

With a rumble and a shake, the tree began to grow before her eyes.

Marie had never seen anything so big.

Then Fritz's toy soldiers sprang to life. They marched in to battle the mice. The mice were led by the fierce and terrible Mouse King, who wore a shiny crown on his head. Then the Nutcracker himself came to life, growing until he was the size of Marie. His bed, now huge, spun around and around.

The Nutcracker leaped out of the bed to lead the battle against the mice. The Mouse King towered over the Nutcracker, taunting him, when a quick-thinking Marie threw her slipper and it landed on the king's head. He turned to look away, and the Nutcracker toppled him over. The Nutcracker triumphantly claimed the Mouse King's crown in victory.

In that very moment, the ancient spell that had been cast on the Nutcracker was broken. He transformed into a handsome prince who looked very much like Herr Drosselmeier's nephew.

The Prince gallantly placed the crown on top of Marie's head and led her by the hand into the starry night, beyond her house and deep into the forest toward the Christmas Star. Snow began to fall, and the glistening flakes began to dance.

The Prince took Marie on a fantastic journey. They boarded a cozy walnut boat and sailed into the night, soon landing in an enchanted kingdom called the Land of Sweets. The Land of Sweets was a magical place filled with candy dripping in icing and magnificent, delicious colors as far as the eye could see.

News of their arrival traveled fast, and Marie and the Prince were greeted by the Sugarplum Fairy, who reigned over the land. She welcomed them with a curtsy, and with a wave of her sparkly wand, a host of delights from her kingdom appeared before them.

The Prince told the story of their great battle with the Mouse King.

"Oh, you are both very brave," the Sugarplum Fairy said. Then she invited them to celebrate by settling in two magnificent candy thrones, with big bowls of chocolate, cake, and ice cream set before them.

The Sugarplum Fairy summoned everyone in the Land of Sweets to dance for the Prince and Marie in honor of their victory.

First there was a delightful dance of spicy Spanish hot chocolate, heralded by the call of trumpets and snapping fingers.

Next came the mysterious Arabian coffee dance that ended with the tinkling of tiny cymbals, giving way to the explosive leaps and turns of Chinese tea.

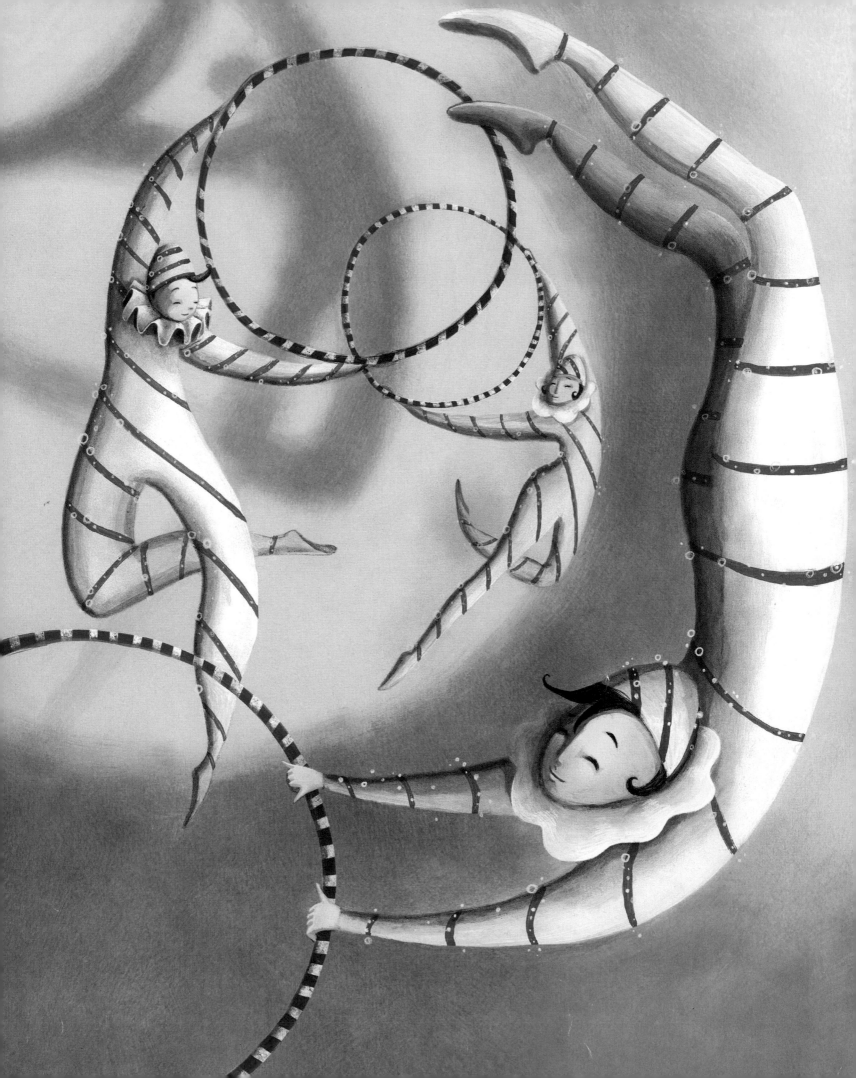

The jumping candy canes emerged next, leaping high into the air and dancing through hoops.

What could come after candy canes? Marzipan shepherdesses stepped out, tiptoeing delicately while playing their flutes.

The biggest surprise of all was the gigantic Mother Ginger, who swaggered before them. All of a sudden eight tiny clowns, called polichinelles, sprang from beneath her skirt and danced to the rhythm of her tambourine.

As Mother Ginger scooted her children off, a garden of flowers appeared. Amid the blooms was the shimmering Dewdrop Fairy, and with each step she brought every single petal to life in blossoming swirls of pink.

Finally, the regal Sugarplum Fairy returned with her noble cavalier. They floated gracefully about, and then she spun faster and faster before leaping into his arms. It was all so deliciously marvelous.

With another wave of her wand, the Sugarplum Fairy summoned her whole kingdom for a joyous farewell celebration.

As much as they wanted to stay, it was time for Marie and the Prince to leave the Land of Sweets and return to their families. As the lovely soft snow continued to fall, they climbed into a beautiful sleigh pulled by magical reindeer. Marie and the Prince turned to wave good-bye to their new friends as they rose higher and higher into the sky, away from their sweet celebration and into the starry night.

George Balanchine's
# THE NUTCRACKER®
## Fun Facts

- The Christmas tree grows to a full height of 41 feet and weighs 1 ton.

- 50 pounds of paper snow is used to create the snowstorm that ends the first act of the ballet.

- There are 144 jingle bells on each of the candy cane costumes.

- Mother Ginger's skirt weighs 85 pounds and is 9 feet wide.

- There are nearly 1 million watts of lighting used in the ballet's grand finale.

- Each performance features more than 50 dancers and more than 60 children from the School of American Ballet, the official school of NYCB.

- More than 150 costumes are worn by the cast.

- 62 musicians play in the orchestra.

*The Nutcracker* was created by composer Peter Ilyitch Tschaikovsky and choreographers Marius Petipa and Lev Ivanov, and it was first performed at the Mariinsky Theater in St. Petersburg, Russia, on December 18, 1892. The ballet was not initially considered a success.

George Balanchine, who was born in St. Petersburg in 1904 and performed in *The Nutcracker* as a student at the Mariinsky Theater, decided to choreograph his own version of the ballet as his first full-length work for New York City Ballet, which he had cofounded in 1948.

Premiering on February 2, 1954, Balanchine's production of *The Nutcracker* was an extraordinary success, and it helped to establish both the ballet and its score as perennial favorites around the world.

## George Balanchine's The Nutcracker®
BALLET IN TWO ACTS, FOUR SCENES, AND PROLOGUE
Based on E. T. A. Hoffmann's tale *The Nutcracker and the Mouse King* (1816)

Music by Peter Ilyitch Tschaikovsky
Choreography by George Balanchine*
Scenery by Rouben Ter-Arutunian
Costumes by Karinska
Original lighting by Ronald Bates
Lighting by Mark Stanley

*© The George Balanchine Trust

Premiere: February 2, 1954, New York City Ballet,
City Center of Music and Drama, New York

Learn more at nycballet.com.